1001 Really
Stupid Jokes

1001 Really Stupid Jokes

Illustrated by Mike Phillips

Robinson Children's Books

First published in the UK by Robinson Children's Books,
an imprint of Constable & Robinson Ltd 2000

Constable & Robinson Ltd
3 The Lanchesters
162 Fulham Palace Road
London W6 9ER

A copy of the British Library Cataloguing-in-Publication Data
is available from the British Library

ISBN 978-1-84119-152-2
ISBN 1-84119-152-3

Printed and bound in the EC

11

Introduction

I smother school dinner with lots of honey.
I've done it all my life.
It makes the food taste funny.
But the peas stay on my knife.

. . . and if you think that's stupid,
just wait . . .

Why is history like a fruit cake?
Because it's full of dates.

What did the mother ghost say to the
naughty baby ghost?
Spook when your spooken to.

Why did Ken keep his trumpet in the fridge?
Because he liked cool music.

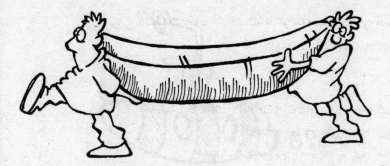

"They're not growing bananas any longer."
"Really? Why not?"
"Because they're long enough already."

"Dad, when I get old will the calves of my legs be cows?"

The wonderful Wizard of Oz
Retired from business becoz
What with up-to-date science
To most of his clients
He wasn't the wizard he woz.

Why didn't the banana snore?
'Cos it was afraid to wake up the rest of the bunch.

Did you hear about the sailor who was discharged from the submarine service?
He was caught sleeping with the windows open.

Why did the stupid sailor grab a bar of soap when his ship sank?
He thought he could wash himself ashore.

An irate woman burst into the baker's shop and said:
"I sent my son in for two pounds of biscuits this morning but when I weighed them there was only one pound. I suggest you check your scales."
The baker looked at her calmly for a moment or two and then replied:
"Madam, I suggest you weigh your son."

An idiotic laborer was told by an equally idiotic foreman to dig a hole in the road.
"And what shall I do with the earth, sir?" asked the laborer.
"Don't be daft, man," he replied. "Just dig another hole and bury it."

Did you hear about the stupid motorist who always drove his car in reverse?
It was because he knew the town backward.

What's the most important thing to remember in chemistry?
Never lick the spoon.

"Waiter, how long have you worked here?"
"Six months, sir."
"Well, it can't have been you who took my order."

"My dad thinks he wears the trousers in our house — but it's always mom who tells him which pair to put on."

"Can you stand on your head?"
"I've tried, but I can't get my feet up high enough."

How do you confuse an idiot?
Give him two spades and ask him to take his pick.

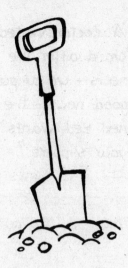

"When you leave school, you should become a bone specialist. You've certainly got the head for it."

Two shark fishermen were sitting on the side of their boat just off the coast of Florida, cooling their feet in the sea. Suddenly an enormous shark swam up and bit off one fisherman's leg.
"A shark's just bitten off my leg," yelled the fisherman.
"Which one?" asked his friend.
"I don't know," replied the first, "when you've seen one shark, you've seen them all."

A doctor visited his patient in the hospital ward after the operation. "I've got some bad news — we amputated the wrong leg. Now the good news — the man in the next bed wants to buy your slippers."

There's a large crack in the sitting room of Jimmy's house so he goes around telling everyone that he's from a broken home.

A stupid bank robber rushed into a bank, pointed two fingers at the clerk and said: "This is a muck up."
"Don't you mean a stick up?" asked the girl.
"No," said the robber, "it's a muck up. I've forgotten my gun."

What happened to the man who couldn't tell the difference between porridge and putty? All his windows fell out.

When Wally Witherspoon proposed to his girlfriend she said:
"I love the simple things in life, Wally, but I don't want one of them for a husband."

Did you hear about the dizzy Boy Scout? He spent all day doing good turns.

What's large and green and sits in a corner on its own all day?
The Incredible Sulk.

"At our local restaurant you can eat dirt cheap – but who wants to eat dirt?"

Knock, Knock.
Who's there?
Armageddon.
Armageddon who?
Armageddon out of here!

Why do surgeons wear masks in the operating theater?
So that if they make a mistake no one will know who did it.

"My son's just
received a scholarship
to medical school —
but they don't
want him while
he's alive."

"What should you do if you swallow a light
bulb?"
"Spit it out and be delighted!"

Did you hear about the millionaire who had
a bad accident?
He fell off his wallet.

What happened to Lady Godiva's horse when
he realized that she wasn't wearing any
clothes?
It made him shy.

Why do vampires never get fat?
They eat necks to nothing.

A woman was in court charged with
wounding her husband. "But madam, why
did you stab him over 100 times?" asked the
judge.
"Oh, your Honor," replied the defendant, "I
didn't know how to switch off the electric
carving knife."

"Doctor, doctor, I think I'm a spoon."
"Sit over there, please, and don't stir."

There was once a puppy called May who loved to pick quarrels with animals who were bigger than she was. One day she argued with a lion. The next day was the first of June.
Why?
Because that was the end of May!

"What do you get if you cross a hedgehog with a giraffe?"
"A long-necked toothbrush."

"Doctor, doctor, my son's just swallowed some gunpowder!"
"Well, don't point him at me."

"Doctor, doctor, Cuthbert keeps biting his nails!"
"That's not serious in a child."
"But Cuthbert bites his toe nails."

What do Paddington Bear and Winnie the Pooh pack for their vacation?
The bear essentials.

"What kind of cats love water?"
"Octopusses."

Britain's oldest lady was 115 years old today, and she hasn't got a gray hair on her head. She's completely bald.

What happens when a band plays in a thunderstorm?
The conductor gets hit by lightning.

What do you get if
you cross a bumble
bee with a
doorbell?
A humdinger.

What does a headless horseman ride?
A nightmare.

Why did the farmer plow his field with a
steamroller?
Because he planned to grow mashed potatoes.

"Doctor, doctor, I think I'm Napoleon."
"How long have you felt like this?"
"Ever since Waterloo."

"What sort of sentence would you get if you broke the law of gravity?"
"A suspended one."

Doctor: "And did you drink your medicine after your bath, Mrs Soap?"
Mrs Soap: "No, doctor. By the time I'd drunk the bath there wasn't room for medicine."

"Doctor, I keep stealing things. What can I do?"
"Try to resist the temptation, but if you can't, get me a new television."

Why does a stork stand on one leg?
Because it would fall over if it lifted the other one.

"Waiter, waiter, this lobster's only got one claw."
"It must have been in a fight, sir."
"Then bring me the winner."

What sort of ship does Count Dracula sail on?
A blood vessel.

Did you hear about Lenny the Loafer?
He is so lazy that he sticks his nose out of the window so that the wind will blow it for him.

Are vampires mad?
Well, they're often bats.

Which day of the week is the strongest?
Sunday — all the rest are "weak" days.

"What's the best place to find diamonds?"
"In a pack of cards."

What's white and flies?
Super Spud.

How did the baker get an electric shock?
He stood on a bun and a current ran up his leg.

"My sister is so stupid she thinks that aroma is someone who travels a lot."

"What fish tastes best with cream?"
"A jellyfish."

"My dad is a real jerk. I told him I needed an encyclopedia for school and he said I'd have to walk just like everyone else!"

"I didn't recognize you for a minute. It was one of the happiest minutes of my life."

"She's such a gossip it doesn't take her long to turn an earful into a mouthful."

Did you hear about the idiotic goalkeeper who saved a penalty but let it in on the action replay?

"Claire's singing is improving. People are putting cotton wool in only one ear now."

"When I was at school I was as smart as the next fellow."
"What a pity the next fellow was such an idiot."

"My dog saw a sign that said: 'Wet Paint' — so he did!"

Why did the idiots' tug o' war team lose the match?
They pushed.

What's a porcupine's favorite food?
Prickled onions.

"Doctor, doctor, my left leg is giving me a lot of pain."
"I expect that's old age."
"But my right leg is as old, and that doesn't hurt at all!"

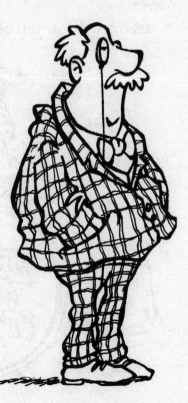

A garbage man was walking along whistling while balancing a bin on his head and one on each shoulder. "How do you manage to do that?" asked Jane.

"It's easy," replied the garbage man. "Just put your lips together and blow."

What's black and white and makes a lot of noise?

A zebra with a set of drums.

George is the type of boy that
his mother doesn't want
him to associate with!

Roger was in a very full bus when a fat
woman opposite said, "If you were a
gentleman, young man, you'd stand up and
let someone else sit down."
"And if you were a lady," replied Roger,
"you'd stand up and let four people sit
down."

A man went into the local department store
where he saw a sign on the escalator – "Dogs
must be carried on this escalator." The silly
man then spent the next two hours looking for
a dog.

"Doctor, doctor, I keep losing my memory."
"When did you first notice that?"
"When did I first notice what?"

Teacher: "If you add 20,567 to 23,678 and then divide by 97 what do you get?"
Jim: "The wrong answer."

"My dog is a nuisance. He chases everyone on a bicycle. What can I do?"
"Take his bike away."

"Little Miss Muffet
Sat on a tuffet
Eating a bowl of stew
Along came a spider
And sat down beside her.
Guess what? She ate him up too!"

Did you hear about the stupid Australian who received a new boomerang for his birthday?
He spent two days trying to throw the old one away.

The seaside resort we went to last year was so boring that one day the tide went out and never came back.

"My Mother uses lemon juice for her complexion."
"Maybe that is why she always looks so sour."

Did you hear about the idiotic karate champion who joined the army?
The first time he saluted, he nearly killed himself.

Boy Monster: "You've got a face like a million dollars."

Girl Monster: "Have I really?"

Boy Monster: "Yes – it's green and wrinkly."

How does an idiot call for his dog?
He puts two fingers in his mouth and then shouts "Rover."

"My girlfriend talks so much that when she goes on holiday, she has to spread suntan lotion on her tongue."

As he was walking along the street the vicar saw a little girl trying to reach a high door knocker. Anxious to help, the vicar went over to her. "Let me do it, dear," he said, rapping the knocker vigorously.

"Great!" said the girl, "Now run like hell."

1st Cannibal: "My dad's so tough he can kill crocodiles with his bare hands."
2nd Cannibal: "My dad's so tough it took six hours in the microwave to cook him."

Chuck: "Do you have holes in your underpants?"
Teacher: "No, of course not."
Chuck: "Then how do you get your feet through?"

What is a snail?
A slug with a crash helmet.

Did you hear about the idiot who made his chickens drink boiling water?
He thought they would lay hard-boiled eggs.

What's thick, black,
floats on water
and shouts
"Knickers!"?
Crude oil.

"Did you thank Mrs Pillbeam for teaching you today?" Alec's mom asked him when he came home from school.
"No I didn't. Mary in front of me did and Mrs Pillbeam said, 'Don't mention it,' so I didn't."

Some people say the school cook's cooking is out of this world.
Most pupils wish it was out of their stomachs.

"At my piano teacher's last performance the audience cheered and cheered. The piano was locked!"

Why was the musician arrested?
For getting into treble.

What's the difference between a bus driver
and a cold in the head?
A bus driver knows the stops, and a cold in
the head stops the nose.

"Waiter, waiter, why is my apple pie all
mashed up?"
"You did ask me to step on it, sir."

Why did the monster eat a light bulb?
Because he was in need of light refreshment.

"Would you say that a cannibal who ate his
mother's sister was an aunt eater?"

A ghost was out haunting one night and met
a fairy fluttering through the forest. "Hello,"
said the ghost. "I've never met a fairy
before. What's your name?"
"Nuff," said the fairy.
"That's a very odd name," said the ghost.
"No, it's not," said the fairy, offended,
"haven't you heard of Fairy Nuff?"

What happened when the cows got out of their field?
There was udder chaos.

A monster went to see the doctor because he kept bumping into things. "You need glasses," said the doctor.
"Will I be able to read with them?" asked the monster.
"Yes."
"That's brilliant," said the monster. "I didn't know how to read before."

The stupid monster went to the mind reader's and paid $5 to have his thoughts read. After half an hour the mind reader gave him his money back.

Knock, knock.
Who's there?
Francis.
Francis who?
Francis a country in Europe.

What do you get if a huge hairy monster
steps on Batman and Robin?
Flatman and Ribbon.

Cross-Eyed Monster: "When
I grow up I want to be
a bus driver."
Witch: "Well, I won't
stand in your way."

How does Jack Frost
get to work?
By icicle.

What should you do if you find a gorilla
sitting at your school desk?
Sit somewhere else.

What did the stupid ghost call his pet tiger?
Spot.

Did you hear about the stupid vampire who
listened to a match?
He burned his ear!

The wizard who had invented
a flying carpet was
interviewed for a local radio
station.
"What's it like, Merlin, to
fly on a magic carpet?"
asked the radio
presenter.
"Rugged," replied
Merlin.

Did you hear about the businessman who is
so rich he has two swimming pools, one of
which is always empty?
It's for people who can't swim!

Why is twice ten the same as twice eleven?
Because twice ten is twenty, and twice eleven
is twenty, too.

Did you hear about the short-sighted monster who fell in love with a piano?
It had such wonderful white teeth, how could he resist it?

Did you hear about the competition to find the laziest spook in the world? All the competitors were lined up on stage. "I've got a really nice, easy job for the laziest person here," said the organizer. "Will the laziest spook raise his hand?"
All the spooks put up their hands — except one.
"Why didn't you raise your hand?" asked the presenter.
"Too much trouble," yawned the spook!

What's an inkling?
A baby fountain pen.

Knock, knock.
Who's there?
Thumping.
Thumping who?
Thumping green and slimy just went up your trousers.

First lion: "Every time I eat, I feel sick."
Second lion: "I know. It's hard to keep a good man down."

Did you hear about the monster who ate bits of metal every night?
It was his staple diet.

What do you get if you cross a cow with a mule?
Milk with a kick in it.

Two Irishmen looking for work saw a sign which read TREE FELLERS WANTED.
"Oh now, look at that," said Paddy. "What a pity there's only de two of us!"

Sharon: "I'm so homesick."
Sheila: "But this is your home!"
Sharon: "I know, and I'm sick of it!"

Did you hear about the woman who was so ugly she could make yogurt by staring at a pint of milk for an hour?

How do you stop a cold
going to your chest?
Tie a knot in your neck.

Sign in a launderette: "Those using automatic
washers should remove their clothes when the
lights go out."

"Mommy, mommy, why do you keep poking
daddy in the ribs?"
"If I don't, the fire will go out."

Why did the elephant cross the road?
To pick up the flattened chicken.

Sign in shop window:
FOR SALE Pedigree bulldog. House trained.
Eats anything. Very fond of children.

"Good news! I've been given a goldfish for my birthday . . . the bad news is that I don't get the bowl until my next birthday!"

"Why do you keep doing the backstroke?"
"I've just had lunch and don't want to swim on a full stomach."

What's the smelliest city in America?
Phew York.

If a dog is tied to a rope 15 feet long, how can it reach a bone 30 feet away?
The rope isn't tied to anything!

"No, no, no!" said the enraged businessman to the persistent salesman. "I cannot see you today!"
"That's fine," said the salesman, "I'm selling spectacles!"

"Please Sir! Please Sir! Why do you keep me locked up in this cage?"
"Because you're the teacher's pet."

"Why are you covered in bruises?"
"I started to walk through a revolving door and then I changed my mind."

A tourist walked into a fish and chip shop in Derry.
"I'll have fish and chips twice," he ordered.
"Sure, I heard you the first time," came the reply.

"Did you hear about the fool who keeps going round saying 'no'?"
"No."
"Oh, so it's you!"

A group of Chinamen who were on safari in Africa came across a pride of lions. "Oh look," said one of the lions. "A Chinese takeaway."

What do you get if you cross a chicken with a cow?
Roost beef.

What did the bookworm say to the school librarian?
"Can I burrow this book please?"

What's a cow's favorite love song?
"When I Fall In Love, It Will Be For Heifer."

"Keep that dog out of my garden. It smells disgusting!" a neighbor said to a small boy one day. The boy went home to tell everyone to stay away from the neighbor's garden because of the smell!

Why couldn't the butterfly go to the dance?
Because it was a moth-ball.

What do you get if you cross an eagle with
a skunk?
A bird that stinks to high heaven.

How can you tell if an elephant has been
sleeping in your bed?
The sheets are wrinkled and the bed smells of
peanuts.

What do you get if you cross a kangaroo
with a sheep?
A woolly jumper.

What has a bottom at the top?
Your legs.

What do you get if you cross a flea with a rabbit?
Bugs Bunny.

What does a caterpillar do on New Year's Day?
Turns over a new leaf.

What do we get from naughty cows?
Bad milk!

What do you get if you cross a crocodile
with a flower?
I don't know, but I'm not going to smell it.

What do you get if you cross a Scottish
legend and a bad egg?
The Loch Ness pongster.

Knock, knock.
Who's there?
Dishes.
Dishes who?
Dishes the way I talk now I've got false
teeth.

What cheese is made backward?
Edam.

What circles a lampshade at 200 mph?
Stirling Moth.

"Doctor, doctor, my husband smells like a fish."
"Poor sole!"

What do you call a multistory pigpen?
A styscraper.

There was a young man called Art,
Who thought he'd be terribly smart,
He ate ten cans of beans,
And busted his jeans,
With a loud and earth-shattering ****!

Why did the pig run away from the pigsty?
He felt that the other pigs were taking him for grunted.

Did you hear about the absent-minded monster who went round and round in a revolving door for three hours?
He didn't know whether he was coming or going!

Why did the sparrow fly into the library?
It was looking for bookworms.

Did you hear about the ghoul's favorite hotel?
It had running rot and mold in every room.

What's yellow and sniffs?
A banana with a bad cold.

What's purple and hums?
A rotten plum!

Did you hear about the boy who sat under a cow?
He got a pat on the head.

"Doctor, how can I cure myself of sleepwalking?"
"Sprinkle tin-tacks on your bedroom floor."

Why are ghosts cowards?
'Cos they've got no guts.

Why did the toad become a lighthouse keeper? He had his own frog-horn.

What does the Indian ghost sleep in? A creepy teepee.

Who brings the monsters their babies? Frankenstork.

What do you think of Dracula films? Fangtastic!

"Doctor, doctor! I feel like a sheep!"
"That's baaaaaad!"

"Doctor, doctor! I feel like an apple!"
"We must get to the core of this."

"Doctor, doctor! I feel like a dog!"
"Sit!"

In which biblical story is tennis
mentioned?
When Moses served in
Pharaoh's court . . .

What did the fireman's
wife get for Christmas?
A ladder in her
stocking.

"I say waiter, there's a fly in my soup!"
"Well, throw him a doughnut — they make super lifebelts!"

Why do elephants have flat feet?
From jumping out of tall trees.

Is the squirt from an elephant's trunk very powerful?
Of course — a jumbo jet can keep 500 people in the air for hours at a time.

How do you make an elephant sandwich?
First of all you get a very large loaf . . .

Why did the cowboy die with his boots on?
'Cos he didn't want to stub his toes when he kicked the bucket.

"Doctor, doctor! I think I need glasses!"
"You certainly do, madam. This is a fish and chip shop."

Carol: "Our teacher gives me the pip."
Darryl: "What's her name?"
Carol: "Miss Lemmon."

What do you call a monster with gravy, meat, and potatoes on his head?
Stew.

What did Tarzan say when he saw the monsters coming?
"Here come the monsters."
And what did he say when he saw the monsters coming with sunglasses on?
Nothing — he didn't recognize them!

If a flying saucer is an aircraft, does that make a flying broomstick a witchcraft?

Science Teacher:
"Can you tell me one
substance that
conducts electricity,
Jane?"
Jane: "Why, er. . ."
Science Teacher:
"Wire is correct."

What do you get if you cross a ghost with a
packet of potato chips?
Snacks that go crunch in the night.

What was Dr Jekyll's favorite game?
Hyde and Seek.

"Waiter, waiter," called a diner at the Monster Café. "There's a hand in my soup." "That's not your soup, sir, that's your finger bowl."

How does Dracula keep fit?
He plays batminton.

Why is a pencil the heaviest thing in your satchel?
Because it's full of lead.

Mrs Jones: "Well, Billy, how are you getting along with your trampolining lessons?"
Billy: "Oh, up and down, you know."

Bob: "Our teacher is very musical you know."
Ben: "Musical? Mr Jenkinson?"
Bob: "Yes. He's always fiddling with his beard."

How do you get a ghost to lie perfectly flat?
You use a spirit level.

Alex and Alan took their lunches to the local cafe to eat.
"Hey!" shouted the proprietor. "You can't eat your own food in here!"
"Okay," said Alex. So he and Alan swapped their sandwiches.

Biology Teacher: "What kinds of birds do we get in captivity?"
Janet: "Jail birds, Miss!"

Teacher: "Are you good at arithmetic?"
Mary: "Well, yes and no."
Teacher: "What do you mean, yes and no?"
Mary: "Yes, I'm no good at arithmetic."

Teacher: "Dennis! When you yawn you
should put your hand to your mouth."
Dennis: "What, and get it bitten?"

Alex's class went on a nature study ramble.
"What do you call a thing with ten legs, red
spots and great big jaws, Sir?" asked Alex.
"I've no idea, why do you ask?" replied the
teacher.
"Because one just crawled up your trouser
leg."

Mandy: "Our teacher went on a special
banana diet."
Andy: "Did she lose weight?"
Mandy: "No, but she couldn't half climb
trees well!"

What were the only creatures not to go into the ark in pairs?
Maggots. They went in an apple.

Why is a classroom like an old car?
Because it's full of nuts, and has a crank at the front.

Art Teacher: "What color would you paint the sun and the wind?"
Brian: "The sun rose, and the wind blue."

When is a blue school book not a blue school book?
When it is read.

When is an English teacher like a judge?
When she hands out long sentences.

Teacher: "Why do you want to work in a bank, Alan?"
Alan: " 'Cos there's money in it, Miss."

Teacher: "Who was that on the phone, Samantha?"
Samantha: "No one important, Miss. Just some man who said it was long distance from Australia, so I told him I knew that already."

What's black and white and horrible?
A math examination paper.

Teacher: "You're wearing a very strange pair of socks, Darren. One's blue with red spots, and one's yellow with green stripes."
Darren: "Yes, and I've got another pair just the same at home."

Teacher: "And did you see the Catskill Mountains on your visit to America?"
Jimmy: "No, but I saw them kill mice."

Where can you dance in California?
San Fran-disco.

Teacher: "Eat up your roast beef, it's full of iron."
Dottie: "No wonder it's so tough."

Two monsters were in hospital and they were discussing their operations and ailments.
"Have you had your feet checked?" one asked the other.
"No," came the reply. "They've always been purple with green spots."

A mother monster marched her naughty little monster into the doctor's surgery. "Is it possible that he could have taken his own tonsils out?" she asked.
"No," said the doctor.
"I told you so," said the mother monster.
"Now, put them back."

What happened when the ice monster had a furious row with the zombie?
He gave him the cold shoulder.

What do you call a teacher floating in the sea?
Bob.

Charlie: "Our school is so old I don't know what stops it from falling down."
Edward: "Maybe the woodworm hold hands."

Why don't ghosts make good magicians?
You can see right through their tricks.

Jim turned up for football practice clutching a large broom.
"What's that for?" asked the coach.
"You said I was going to be sweeper today."

Geography Teacher: "What mineral is exported from America?"
Daft Darren: "Coca-Cola!"

What did the dinner lady say when the teacher told her off for putting her finger in his soup?
"It's all right, it isn't hot."

How many vampires can you fit into an empty sports stadium?
One – after that it's not empty.

"Ann! Point out Australia for me on the map."

Ann went to the front of the class, picked up the pointer and showed the rest of the class where Australia was.

"Well done! Now, Jim! Can you tell us who discovered Australia?"

"Er . . . Ann, Miss?"

Teacher: "You weren't at school last Friday, Robert. I heard you were out playing football."

Robert: "That's not true, Sir. And I've got the cinema tickets to prove it."

What do you call a skeleton who goes out in the snow and rain without a coat or an umbrella?
A numbskull.

What did the werewolf eat after he'd had his teeth taken out?
The dentist.

I'm not saying our teacher's fat, but every time she falls over she rocks herself to sleep trying to get back up.

Monster: "I've got to walk 25 miles home."
Ghost: "Why don't you take a train?"
Monster: "I did once, but my mother made me give it back."

Which space movie stars Count Dracula?
The Vampire Strikes Back.

"Mommy, mommy, what's a vampire?"
"Be quiet, dear, and drink your soup before it clots."

"Jean, define a baby."
"A soft pink thing that makes a lot of noise at one end and has no sense of responsibility at the other."

"Mary," said her teacher. "You can't bring
that lamb into school. What about the
smell?"
"Oh, that's all right, Miss," said Mary. "It'll
soon get used to it."

What did Frankenstein's monster say when he
was struck by lightning?
"Thanks, I needed that."

Why is the school swot like quicksand?
Because everything in school sinks into him.

I used to be thin.
Now I'm thinner.
So would you be
With our school dinner.

What are pupils at ghost schools called?
Ghoulboys and ghoulgirls.

Two schoolboys were talking about their
arithmetic lessons.
"Why do you suppose we stop the tables at
12?" asked one.
"Oh, don't you know," said the other. "I
heard Mom say it was unlucky to have 13 at
table."

"Teacher is a bore!" was scrawled on the
blackboard one day.
"I do not want to see that on my
blackboard," he thundered when he saw it.
"Sorry, Sir! I didn't realize you wanted it
kept secret."

Was the carpenter's son a chip off the old block?

Why wouldn't the skeleton go to school?
Because his heart wasn't in it.

Harry: "Please may I have another pear, Miss?"
Teacher: "Another, Harry? They don't grow on trees, you know."

"Lie flat on your backs, class, and circle your feet in the air as if you were riding your bikes" said the gym teacher.
"Jim! What are you doing? Move your feet, boy."
"I'm freewheeling, Sir."

"Jim," groaned his father when he saw his son's school report. "Why are you so awful at geography?"
"It's the teacher's fault, Dad. He keeps telling us about places I've never heard of."

Did you hear about the schoolboy who just couldn't get to grips with decimals?
He couldn't see the point.

What's the difference between teachers and candy?
People like candy.

Why is it bad to upset a cannibal?
You end up in hot water.

"Why are you crying, Jim?" asked the teacher.

"'Cos my parrot died last night. I washed it in Persil."

"Jim," said the teacher. "You must have known that Persil's bad for parrots."

"Oh it wasn't the Persil that killed it, Sir. It was the spin drier."

What's the difference between a railway guard and a teacher?

One minds the train, the other trains the mind.

"Jim," said the religious education teacher, "you've written here that Samson was an actor. What makes you think that?"

"Well Sir," said Jim, "I read that he brought the house down."

Why did the singing teacher have such a high-pitched voice?

She had falsetto teeth.

"And what might your name be?" the school secretary asked the new boy.
"Well it might be Cornelius, but it's not. It's Sam."

What happened to the baby chicken that misbehaved at school?
It was eggspelled.

"I don't care who you are, get those reindeer off my roof."

Why don't centipedes play football?
Because by the time they've
got their boots on it's time
to go home.

Teacher: "Can anyone tell me what a
shamrock is?"
Jimmy: "It's a fake diamond, Miss."

"Ann," said the dancing mistress. "There
are two things stopping you becoming the
world's greatest ballerina."
"What are they, Miss?" asked Ann.
"Your feet."

"My dad is so short-sighted he can't get to sleep unless he counts elephants."

Why did the football teacher give his team lighters?
Because they kept losing all their matches.

Donald: "My canary died of flu."
Dora: "I didn't know canaries got flu."
Donald: "Mine flew into a car."

Why was the principal not pleased when he bumped into an old friend?
They were both driving their cars at the time.

"That's an excellent essay for someone your age," said the English teacher.
"How about for someone my Mom's age, Miss?"

"Well, children," said the cannibal cookery teacher. "What did you make of the new English teacher?"
"Burgers, Miss."

What's the difference between school dinners and a bucket of fresh manure?
School dinners are usually cold.

Did you hear about the little spook who couldn't sleep at night because his brother kept telling him human stories?

How do fleas travel from place to place?
By itch hiking.

What did they say about the aristocratic monster?

That he was born with a silver shovel in his mouth.

What happens if you tell a psychiatrist you are schizophrenic?

He charges you double.

If you watch the way that many motorists drive you will soon reach the conclusion that the most dangerous part of a car is the nut behind the wheel.

Why did the lady monster wear curlers at night?
She wanted to wake up curly in the morning.

"Do you serve women in this bar?"
"No sir, you have to bring your own."

"I don't know what it is that makes you stupid but whatever it is, it works."

Why was the sword-swallowing monster put in prison?
He coughed and killed two people.

A man who forgets his wife's birthday is certain to get something to remember her by.

Did you hear about the man who ate 106 cloves of garlic a day?
He was taken to hospital in a coma. Doctors said it was from inhaling his own breath.

"Doctor, doctor, I'm nervous, this is the first brain operation I've had."
"Don't worry, it's the first I've performed."

What happens if you play table tennis with a bad egg?
First it goes ping, then it goes pong.

What's the difference between a coyote and a flea?
One howls on the prairie, and the other prowls on the hairy.

"Doctor, doctor, I've got a little stye."
"Then you'd better buy a little pig."

What did the zombie say when he knocked on Eddie's door?
"Eddie body home?"

Who is Wyatt Burp?
The sheriff with the repeater.

Golfer: "Caddy, why do you keep looking at your watch?"
Caddy: "It's not a watch, it's a compass."

What is small, pink, wrinkly, and belongs to Grandpa?
Grandma.

What do you get if you cross a witch with
an ice cube?
A cold spell.

Teacher: "Are you really going to leave
school, Ben, or are you just saying that to
brighten my day?"

Did you hear about the time Eddy's sister
tried to make a birthday cake?
The candles melted in the oven.

"My dad is rather tired this morning. Last night he dreamed he was working."

Did you hear about the horrible hairy monster who did farmyard impressions?
He didn't do the noises, he just made the smells.

Why are school cooks cruel?
Because they batter fish and beat eggs.

What's the best thing to put into a pizza?
Your teeth.

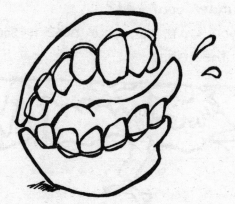

Knock, knock.
Who's there?
Bella.
Bella who?
Bella not working, that's why I knocka.

Why did the stupid pilot land his plane on a house?
Because the landing lights were on.

"How do you make someone burn his ear?"
"Ring him up when he is ironing."

How do you know when there's a monster hiding under your bed?
When you wake up, your nose is squashed up against the ceiling.

Where do witches' frogs sit?
On toadstools.

First Woman: "Whenever I'm down in the dumps I buy myself a new hat."
Second Woman: "Oh, so that's where you get them."

Wife: "Shall I give that tramp one of my cakes?"
Husband: "Why, what harm has he ever done us?"

What did the Eskimo children sing when their principal was leaving?
Freeze a Jolly Good Fellow.

My uncle is the meanest man in the world. He recently found a crutch — then he broke his leg so he could use it.

"My uncle spent a fortune on deodorants before he found out that people didn't like him anyway."

"It was so hot when we went on holiday last year that we had to take turns sitting in each other's shadow."

"I can't understand the critics saying that only an idiot would like that television program. I really enjoyed it."

What's the difference between a schoolteacher and a train?
A schoolteacher says, "Spit out that toffee" and a train says, "Choo, choo."

Why don't you go home and brush up on your ignorance?

Teacher: "Who can tell me where Turkey is?"
Dumb Donald: "We ate ours last Thanksgiving, Miss."

What's the difference between a
vampire and a biscuit?
You can't dip a vampire in
your tea.

Did you hear about the ogre who threw
trunks over cliffs?
Nothing special about that, you might think —
but the elephants were still attached.

What's the best way of stopping a monster
sliding through the eye of a needle?
Tie a knot in his neck.

Why did the monster drink ten liters of anti-
freeze?
So that he didn't have to buy a winter coat.

Why does Dracula always travel with his
coffin?
Because his life is at stake.

Knock, knock.
Who's there?
Gopher.
Gopher who?
Gopher a walk over the cliff.

What's a giant's favorite tale?
A tall story.

What did the monster say when he saw
Santa Claus?
"Yum, yum."

"I reckon Mom must be at least 30 years old
— I counted the rings under her eyes."

When Dad came home he was astonished to see Susie sitting on a horse, writing something. "What on earth are you doing there?" he asked.

"Well, teacher told us to write an essay on our favorite animal. That's why I'm here and that's why Jim's standing in the goldfish bowl."

Why did the teacher call both her children Ed?
Because she thought two Eds were better than one.

Why did the school orchestra have bad manners?
Because it didn't know how to conduct itself.

Robot: "I have to dry my feet carefully after a bath."
Monster: "Why?"
Robot: "Otherwise I get rusty nails."

Caspar: "I was the teacher's pet last year."
Jaspar: "Why was that?"
Caspar: "She couldn't afford a dog."

Why was the student witch so bad at essays?
Because she couldn't spell properly.

"My sister thinks that a juggernaut is an empty beer mug."

Janet came home from school and asked her mother if the aerosol spray in the kitchen was hair lacquer.

"No," said Mom. "It's glue."

"I thought so," said Janet. "I wondered why I couldn't get my hat off today."

Why is it difficult to open a piano?
Because all the keys are inside.

Knock, knock.
Who's there?
Alison.
Alison who?
Alison to my teacher!

Did you hear about the boy who had to do a project on trains?
He had to keep track of everything!

How do you stop a werewolf howling in the back of a car?
Put him in the front.

How can a teacher increase the size of her pay check?
By looking at it through a magnifying glass.

Ben's teacher regards Ben as a wonder child.
He wonders whether he'll ever learn anything.

"I've got a good idea."
"Must be beginner's luck."

What kind of ghosts haunt hospitals?
Surgical spirits.

Geography Teacher: "What is the coldest place in the world?"
Ann: "Chile."

Dim Dinah wrote in her exercise book:
Margarine is butter made from imitation cows.

Which day of the week do ghosts like best?
Moandays.

How do hens dance?
Chick to chick.

Why wouldn't the skeleton go to the ghoul's school disco?
He had no body to go with.

Did you hear about the cross-eyed teacher?
She had no control over her pupils.

What's the longest piece of furniture in the
school?
The multiplication table.

Miss Jones who teaches us math,
Isn't much of a laugh.
For, sad to tell,
She doesn't half smell,
For she never has taken a bath.

What did the arithmetic book say to the
geometry book?
Boy! Do we have our problems!

Did you hear what happened when there was
an epidemic of laryngitis at school?
The school nurse sent everyone to the
croakroom.

The games teacher, Miss Janet Rockey,
Wanted to train as a jockey.
But, sad to recall,
She grew far too tall.
So now she teaches us hockey.

"Welcome to school, Simon," said the nursery school teacher to the new boy. "How old are you?"
"I'm not old," said Simon. "I'm nearly new."

"Please Miss!" said a little boy at kindergarten. "We're going to play elephants and circuses, do you want to join in?"
"I'd love to," said the teacher. "What do you want me to do?"
"You can be the lady that feeds us peanuts!"

What's the difference between an angler and a schoolboy?
One baits his hooks. The other hates his books.

"Why are you crying, Amanda?" asked her teacher.
" 'Cos Jenny's broken my new doll, Miss," she cried.
"How did she do that?"
"I hit her on the head with it."

What do you get if you cross old potatoes
with lumpy mince?
School dinners.

The night-school teacher asked one of his
pupils when he had last sat an exam.
"1945," said the lad.
"Good lord! That's more than 40 years ago."
"No Sir! An hour and half, it's quarter past
nine now."

"I'd like you to be very quiet today, boys
and girls. I've got a dreadful headache."
"Please Miss!" said Jim. "Why don't you do
what Mom does when she has a headache?"
"What's that?"
"She sends us out to play."

Games mistress: "Come on, Sophie. You can
run faster than that."
Sophie: "I can't, Miss. I'm wearing run-
resistant tights."

Confucius he say: If teacher ask you question
and you not know answer, mumble.

Why was the little bird expelled from school?
She was always playing practical yolks.

A little girl was next in line. "My
name's Curtain," she said.
"I hope your first name's not Annette."
"No. It's Velvet."

"And what's your name?" the secretary asked the next new boy.
"Butter."
"I hope your first name's not Roland," smirked the secretary.
"No, Miss. It's Brendan."

"Who was Captain Kidd?" asked the history teacher.
"He was a contortionist."
"What makes you think that, Jim?"
"Well it says in the history book that he spent a lot of time sitting on his chest."

Did you hear about the math teacher who fainted in class?
Everyone tried to bring her 2.

Knock, knock.
Who's there?
Canoe.
Canoe who?
Canoe help me with my homework, please, Dad. I'm stuck.

What do you call an English teacher, five feet tall, covered from head to toe in boils and totally bald?
Sir!

"Teacher reminds me of the sea," said Jim to Billy.
"You mean she's deep, sometimes calm but occasionally stormy?"
"No! She makes me sick."

Why did the math teacher take a ruler to bed with him?
He wanted to see how long he would sleep.

Did you hear about the Irish schoolboy who was studying Greek Mythology?
When the teacher asked him to name something that was half-man and half-beast he replied, "Buffalo Bill."

When the school was broken into, the thieves took absolutely everything – desks, books, blackboards, everything apart from the soap in the lavatories and all the towels.
The police are looking for a pair of dirty criminals.

Teacher: "That's the stupidest boy in the whole school."
Mother: "That's my son."
Teacher: "Oh! I'm so sorry."
Mother: "You're sorry!"

What's the difference between a boring teacher and a boring book?
You can shut the book up.

Typing teacher: "Bob! Your work has certainly improved. There are only ten mistakes here."
Bob: "Oh good, Miss."
Teacher: "Now let's look at the second line, shall we?"

Why is a man wearing sunglasses like a rotten teacher?
Because he keeps his pupils in the dark.

Why are some teachers jealous of driving instructors?
Because driving instructors are allowed to belt their pupils.

Did you hear about the brilliant geography master?
He had abroad knowledge of his subject.

The headmaster was interviewing a new teacher.

"You'll get $10,000 to start, with $15,000 after six months."

"Oh!" said the teacher. "I'll come back in six months then."

The schoolteacher was furious when Jim knocked him down with his new bicycle in the playground.

"Don't you know how to ride that yet?" he roared.

"Oh yes!" shouted Jim over his shoulder. "It's the bell I can't work yet."

"What do you do?" a man asked a very attractive girl at a party.
"I'm an infant teacher."
"Good gracious! I thought you were at least 26."

"You never get anything right," complained the teacher. "What kind of job do you think you'll get when you leave school?"
"Well I want to be the weather girl on TV."

"Jim won't be at school today," said his mother on the telephone. "He's broken an arm."

"Well tell him we hope he gets better soon."

"Oh he's fine now," said the mother. "It was my arm he broke."

"Please Sir. There's something wrong with my stomach."

"Well button up your jacket and no one will notice."

Why are art galleries like retirement homes for teachers?

Because they're both full of old masters.

A warning to any young sinner,
Be you fat or perhaps even thinner.
If you do not repent,
To Hell you'll be sent.
With nothing to eat but school dinner.

Why did the flea fail his exams?
He wasn't up to scratch.

"I asked you to draw a pony and trap,"
said the art master. "You've only drawn the
pony. Why?"
"Well, Sir, I thought the pony would draw
the trap."

"Did you know that eight out of ten
schoolchildren use ballpoint pens to write
with?"
"Gosh! What do the other two use them for?"

"I'm not going to school today," Alexander
said to his mother. "The teachers bully me
and the boys in my class don't like me."
"You're going. And that's final. I'll give you
two good reasons why."
"Why?"
"Firstly, you're 35 years old. Secondly, you're
the principal."

"Your pupils must miss you a lot," said the woman in the next bed to the teacher in hospital.
"Not at all! Their aim's usually good. That's why I'm here."

"I did not come into the classroom to listen to you lot being impertinent," complained the teacher.
"Oh! Where do you usually go, Miss?"

What subject are witches good at in school?
English! Because they're the tops at spelling.

How do you keep a stupid person happy for hours?
Give him a piece of paper with PTO written on both sides.

"I have decided to abolish all corporal punishment at this school," said the principal at morning assembly. "That means that there will be no physical punishment."
"Does that mean that you're stopping school dinners as well, Sir?"

"Please, Miss! How do you spell 'ichael'?"
The teacher was rather bewildered. "Don't
you mean Michael?"
"No Miss. I've written the 'M' already."

"What did the doctor say to you yesterday?"
asked the teacher.
"He said I was allergic to horses."
"I've never heard of anyone suffering from
that. What's the condition called?"
"Bronco-itis."

Teacher's strong; teacher's gentle.
Teacher's kind. And I am mental.

The teacher was furious with her son. "Just
because you've been put in my class, there's
no need to think you can take liberties. You're
a pig."
The boy said nothing.
"Well! Do you know what a pig is?"
"Yes Mom," said the boy. "The offspring of a
swine."

A gym teacher who came from Quebec,
Wrapped both legs around his neck.
But sad, he forgot
How to untie the knot
And now he's a highly-strung wreck.

Why did the teacher have her hair in a bun?
Because she had her nose in a hamburger.

"I was doing my homework yesterday and I
asked my dad what a circle is. He said it's
a round straight line with a hole in the
middle."

Why is the stupid red-headed boy like a
biscuit?
Because he's a ginger nut.

It's obvious that animals are smarter than
humans. Put eight horses in a race and
20,000 people will go along to see it. But put
eight people in a race and not one horse will
bother to go along and watch.

Eddy's father called up to him: "Eddy, if you don't stop playing that trumpet I think I'll go crazy."

"I think you are already," replied Eddy. "I stopped playing half an hour ago."

One day Bob's mother turned to Bob's father and said, "It's such a nice day, I think I'll take Bob to the zoo."

"I wouldn't bother," said father. "If they want him, let them come and get him."

Did you hear about the man who hijacked a submarine?
He demanded a million dollars and a parachute.

Jane's father decided to take all the family out to a restaurant for a meal. As he'd spent quite a lot of money for the meal he said to the waiter, "Could I have a bag to take the leftovers home for the dog?"
"Gosh!" exclaimed Jane. "Are we getting a dog?"

Why is it that when I stand on my head the blood rushes to my head but when I stand on my feet the blood doesn't rush to my feet? You're feet aren't empty.

Why did the stupid person give up his attempt to cross the Channel on a plank?
He couldn't find a plank that was long enough.

Beautician: "Did that mud pack I gave you for your wife improve her appearance?"
Man: "It did for a while – then it fell off."

Jim: "Our dog is just like one of the family."
Fred: "Which one?"

What is black, gushes out of the ground and shouts "Excuse me"?
Refined oil.

A stupid glazier was examining a broken window. He looked at it for a while and then said: "It's worse than I thought. It's broken on both sides."

"Our librarian is so stupid she thinks that an autobiography is a book about the life story of a car."

Roger is so lazy that when he drops something he waits till he has to tie his shoelaces before he'll pick it up.

Girl: "Did you like that cake, Mrs Jones?"
Mrs Jones: "Yes, very much."
Girl: "That's funny. My mom said you didn't have any taste."

Why did the robot act stupid?
Because he had a screw loose.

My sister is so dim she thinks that a cartoon
is a song you sing in a car.

Mary had a bionic cow,
It lived on safety pins.
And every time she milked that cow
The milk came out in tins.

Did you hear about the florist who had two children?
One's a budding genius and the other's a blooming idiot.

Neil: "I've changed my mind."
Jim: "About time, too. Does the new one work any better?"

Did you hear about the man who tried to iron his curtains?
He fell out of the window.

Why did the monster have to buy two tickets for the zoo?
One to get in and one to get out.

"Doctor, doctor, I've just swallowed the film from my camera."
"Well, let's hope nothing develops."

"Doctor, doctor, I think I'm invisible."
"Who said that?"

1st Monster: "That gorgeous four-eyed creature just rolled her eyes at me!"
2nd Monster: "Well, roll them back again — she might need them."

What's a cannibal's favorite game?
Swallow my leader.

What do you get if you cross a galaxy with a toad?
Star Warts.

A woman woke her husband in the middle of the night. "There's a burglar downstairs eating the cake that I made this morning."
"Who shall I call," her husband said, "police or ambulance?"

"My mother is so stupid that she thinks a string quartet is four people playing tennis."

"That boy is so dirty, the only time he washes his ears is when he eats watermelon."

"My friend is so stupid that he thinks twice before saying nothing."

Which bird is always out of breath?
A puffin.

What do you get if you pour hot water down a rabbit hole?
Hot cross bunnies!

On which side does a chicken have the most feathers?
On the outside.

"You should get a job in the meteorology office."
"Why?"
"Because you're an expert on wind."

1st Monster: "I'm so thirsty my tongue's hanging out."
2nd Monster: "Oh, I thought it was your tie!"

What did ET's mother say to him when he got home?
"Where on Earth have you been?"

What time is it when a monster sits on your car?
Time to get a new car.

A man telephoned London Airport. "How long does it take to get to New York?"
"Just a minute."
"Thanks very much."

Brian: "How did you manage to get a black eye?"
Bertie: "You see that tree in the playground?"
Brian: "Yes."
Bertie: "Well, I didn't."

Teacher: "What is the longest night of the year?"
Alex: "A fortnight."

Why are monsters' fingers never more than 11 inches long?
Because if they were 12 inches, they would be a foot.

What do you get if you cross a zombie with a Boy Scout?
A creature that scares old ladies across the road.

"Waiter, waiter, have you got frogs' legs?"
"No Sir, I always walk like this."

Teacher: "Recite your tables to me, Joan."
Joan: "Dining-room table, kitchen table, bedside table . . ."

What's the best way to avoid being troubled
by biting insects?
Don't bite any!

Why did the teacher fix her bed to the
chandelier?
Because she was a light sleeper.

What should you do if you find yourself
surrounded by Dracula, Frankenstein, a zombie
and a werewolf?
Hope you're at a fancy dress party.

A school inspector was talking to a pupil.
"How many teachers work in this school?" he asked.
"Only about half of them, I reckon," replied the pupil.

Teacher: "What's the difference between a buffalo and a bison?"
Student: "You can't wash your hands in a buffalo, Miss."

Why should a school not be near a chicken farm?
To avoid the pupils overhearing fowl language.

Ben, sniffing: "Smells like UFO for dinner tonight, chaps."
Ken: "What's UFO?"
Ben: "Unidentified Frying Objects."

Dave: "The trouble with our teachers is that they all do bird impressions."
Mave: "Really? What do they do?"
Dave: "They watch us like hawks."

Tracy: "Would you punish someone for something they haven't done?"
Teacher: "Of course not."
Tracy: "Oh good, because I haven't done my homework."

A teacher went into a shoe shop. "I'd like some crocodile shoes, please," she said. "Certainly, Madam," said the salesgirl. "How big is your crocodile?"

Teacher: "Martin, put some more water in the fish tank."
Martin: "But, Sir, they haven't drunk the water I gave them yesterday."

Teacher: "Andrew, your homework looks as if it is in your father's handwriting."
Andrew: "Well, I used his pen, Sir."

Father: "Would you like me to help you with your homework?"
Son: "No thanks, I'd rather get it wrong by myself."

What should you give short elves?
Elf-raising flour.

Why did the headmistress put wheels on her rocking chair?
She liked to rock and roll.

Why does the Hound of the Baskervilles turn round and round before he lies down for the night?
Because he's the watchdog and he has to wind himself up.

Statistics say that one in three people is mentally ill. So check your friends and if two of them seem okay, you're the one.

Piano Tuner: "I've come to tune the piano."
Music Teacher: "But we didn't send for you."
Piano Tuner: "No, but the people who live across the street did."

Good news — two boys went out one day climbing trees.
Bad news — one of them fell out.
Good news — there was a hammock beneath him.
Bad news — there was a rake beside the hammock.
Good news — he missed the rake.
Bad news — he missed the hammock too.

What do you get if you cross a frog with a decathlete?
Someone who pole vaults without a pole.

Who wrote Count Dracula's life story?
The ghost writer.

Where does Dracula keep his savings?
In the blood bank.

Why can't the deaf teacher be sent to
prison?
Because you can't condemn someone without
a hearing.

Did you hear about the monster who was
known as Captain Kirk?
He had a left ear, a right ear and a final
front ear.

What did one of Frankenstein's ears say to
the other?
I didn't know we were living on the same
block.

How can you drop an egg six feet without
breaking it?
By dropping it seven feet —
it won't break for the
first six.

"Mommy, mommy, teacher keeps saying I look like a werewolf."
"Be quiet dear and go and comb your face."

A monster went shopping with sponge fingers in one ear and jelly and custard in the other.
"Why have you got jelly and custard and sponge fingers in your ears?" asked the shop assistant.
"You'll have to speak up," said the monster.
"I'm a trifle deaf."

What kind of beans do cannibals like best?
Human beans.

"Doctor, doctor, my wife thinks she's a duck."
"You better bring her in to see me straight away."
"I can't do that — she's already flown south for the winter."

Why is school like a shower?
One wrong turn and you're in hot water.

Did you hear about the burglar who fell in the cement mixer?
Now he's a hardened criminal.

Why did the huge horrible monster go to see the psychiatrist?
Because he was worried that people liked him.

Igor: "Only this morning Dr Frankenstein completed another amazing operation. He crossed an ostrich with a centipede."
Dracula: "And what did he get?"
Igor: "We don't know — we haven't managed to catch it yet."

Why did the monster jump up and down?
Because he'd just taken his medicine and
he'd forgotten to shake the bottle.

Did you hear about the utterly brainless
monster who sat on the floor?
He fell off.

Did you hear about the skeleton which was
attacked by the dog?
It ran off with some bones and left him
without a leg to stand on.

Why did the monster take his nose apart?
To see what made it run.

What's the best thing to give a seasick
elephant?
Plenty of room.

Why was the mother kangaroo cross with her
children?
Because they ate fries in bed.

How does a Clever Dick spend hours on his homework every night, and yet get twelve hours' sleep?
He puts his homework underneath his mattress.

The principal was taking her class round an art gallery. She stopped in front of one exhibit, and sneered at the guide, "I suppose that is some kind of modern art?"
"No, madam," replied the guide. "I'm afraid it's a mirror."

A monster decided to become a TV star, so he went to see an agent. "What do you do?" asked the agent.

"Bird impressions," said the monster.

"What kind of bird impressions?"

"I eat worms."

Did you hear about the two fat men who ran in the New York Marathon?

One ran in short bursts, the other in burst shorts!

What's the easiest way to make a banana split?

Cut it in half.

How do we know that Rome was built at night?
Because all the books say it wasn't built in a day!

What is the most popular sentence at school?
I don't know.

Did you hear about the two little boys who found themselves in a modern art gallery by mistake?
"Quick," said one, "run! Before they say we did it!"

Just before the Ark set sail, Noah saw his two sons fishing over the side. "Go easy on the bait, lads," he said. "Remember I've only got two worms."

And what goes into the water pink and comes out blue?
A swimmer on a cold day!

Why do barbers make good drivers?
Because they know all the short cuts.

Did you hear about the idiot who had a new bath put in?

The plumber said, "Would you like a plug for it?"

The idiot replied, "Oh, I didn't know it was electric."

What happened to the man who put his false teeth in backwards?

He ate himself!

Cannibal Boy: "I've brought a friend home for dinner."

Cannibal Mom: "Put him in the fridge and we'll have him tomorrow."

What happened to the tailor who made his trousers from sun-blind material?

Every time the sun came out, the trousers rolled down.

Pupil: "Excuse me sir, but I don't think I deserve a mark of zero for this exam paper."

Teacher: "Neither do I, but it's the lowest mark I can give."

"Why did you drop the baby?"
"Well, Mrs Smith said he was a bonny bouncing baby, so I wanted to see if he did."

What is a dimple?
A pimple going the wrong way.

What's the difference between a square peg in a round hole and a kilo of lard?
One's a fat lot of good and the other's a good lot of fat!

What's hairy and damp and sits shivering at fairs?
A coconut with a cold.

What sort of fish performs surgical operations?
A sturgeon.

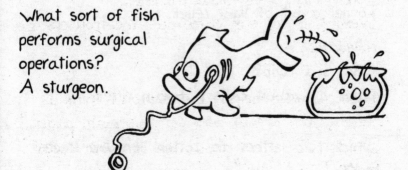

Why did the teacher decide to become an electrician?
To get a bit of light relief.

What's a twip?
What a wabbit calls a twain ride!

Which two letters are rotten for your teeth?
D K

What did the monster say when he saw
Snow White and the Seven Dwarfs?
"Yum, yum!"

Kelly: "Is God a doctor, Miss?"
Teacher: "In some ways, Kelly. Why do you
ask?"
Kelly: "Because the Bible says that the Lord
gave the tablets to Moses."

What did the werewolf write at the bottom
of the letter?
Best vicious . . .

"Waiter, waiter, there's a dead beetle in my
gravy."
"Yes, sir. Beetles are terrible swimmers."

Keith: "Our teacher's an old bat."
Kevin: "You mean he's bad-tempered?"
Keith: "Not only that, he hangs around us all
the time."

The Stock Market is a place where sheep and
cattle are sold.

What happened when the werewolf met the five-headed monster?
It was love at first fright.

What did the speak-your-weight machine say when the fat lady stepped on?
"One at a time, please."

Sign on the school noticeboard: Guitar for sale, cheap, no strings attached.

What happened to Ray when he met the man-eating monster?
He became an ex-Ray.

What's a skeleton's favorite musical instrument?
A trombone.

Darren, at school dinner: "I've just swallowed a bone."
Teacher: "Are you choking?"
Darren: "No, I'm serious."

Girl: "Shall I put the kettle on?"
Boy: "No, I think you look all right in the dress you're wearing."

Mary's class was taken to the Natural History Museum in London.
"Did you enjoy yourself?" asked her mother when she got home.
"Oh yes," replied Mary. "But it was funny going to a dead zoo."

First Teacher: "What's wrong with young Jimmy today? I saw him running round the playground screaming and pulling at his hair!"
Second Teacher: "Don't worry. He's just lost his marbles."

What does the music teacher do when he's locked out of the classroom?
Sing until he gets the right key.

Miss Smith and Mrs Brown were having a chat over a cup of tea about why they entered the teaching profession. "I used to be a fortune teller before I became a teacher," said Miss Smith. "But I had to give it up, there wasn't any future in it."

What do you get when you cross an idiot with a watch?
A cuckoo clock.

Sign outside the school caretaker's

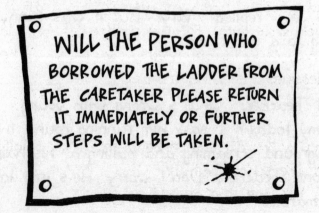

WILL THE PERSON WHO BORROWED THE LADDER FROM THE CARETAKER PLEASE RETURN IT IMMEDIATELY OR FURTHER STEPS WILL BE TAKEN.

What do you get if you cross a caretaker
with a monk who smokes large cigars?
A caretaker with a bad habit.

Why was Harold called the space cadet
when he was at school?
Because he had a lot of space between his
ears.

Retired colonel, talking of the good old
days: "Have you ever hunted bear?"
His grandson's teacher: "No, but I've been
fishing in shorts."

Mrs Turbot, the biology teacher, was very
fond of fish. She was also rather deaf,
which was great for the children in her class.
"What Mrs Turbot needs," said one of her
colleagues, "is a herring-aid."

What's the difference between an iced lolly
and the school bully?
You lick one, the other licks you.

Did you hear about the schoolboy who was so lazy he went around with his mouth open to save him the trouble of yawning?

Games Master: "Why didn't you stop the ball?"
Hapless Harold: "I thought that was what the net was for."

Nigel: "You said the school dentist would be painless, but he wasn't."
Teacher: "Did he hurt you?"
Nigel: "No, but he screamed when I bit his finger."

Igor: "How was that science fiction movie you saw last night?
Dr Frankenstein: "Oh, the same old story – boy meets girl, boy loses girl, boy builds new girl . . ."

Teacher: "What do you know about Lake Erie?"
Rose: "It's full of ghosts, Miss."

Which animals were the last to leave the ark?
The elephants — they were packing their trunks.

Dr Frankenstein: "How can I stop that monster charging?"
Igor: "Why not take away his credit card?"

Did you hear about the vain monster who was going bald?
The doctor couldn't do a hair transplant for him so he shrunk his head to fit his hair.

The monster from outer space decided to go on a trip around the universe, so he went to the rocket office to book a ticket to the moon. "Sorry, sir," said the attendant, "the moon is full at the moment."

Why was the cannibal expelled from school?
Because he kept buttering up the teacher.

What should you call a polite, friendly, kind, good-looking monster?
A failure.

Teacher: "Name six things that contain milk."
Daft Dora: "Custard, cocoa, and four cows."

Brian: "Our school must have very clean kitchens."
Bill: "How can you tell?"
Brian: "All the food tastes of soap."

What has two heads, three hands, two noses and five feet?
A monster with spare parts.

"I have two noses, three eyes and only one ear. What am I?"
"Very ugly."

What is a man who tests people's eyes called?
An optimist.

Why is a caretaker nothing like Robinson Crusoe?
Because Robinson Crusoe got all his work done by Friday.

A teacher took her class for a walk in the country, and Susie found a grass snake.
"Come quickly, Miss," she called, "here's a tail without a body!"

"Waiter, do you serve crabs?"
"Sit down, sir. We serve anybody."

Why did the old lady cover her mouth with her hands when she sneezed?
To catch her false teeth.

Why did the man go out and buy a set of tools?
Because everyone kept telling him he had a screw loose.

Teacher to Dinner Lady: "A pork chop, please and make it lean."
Dinner Lady: "Certainly, Mr Smith, which way?"

Wilberforce Witherspoon saw a notice outside a police station which read: MAN WANTED FOR ROBBERY. So he went in and applied for the job!

Why did the music student have a piano in the bathroom?
Because he was practising Handel's "Water Music."

How do you catch a squirrel?
Climb up a tree and act like a nut.

Simple Simon was writing a geography essay. It began, "The people who live in Paris are called parasites . . ."

There was a fight in the fish shop last night – a whole lot of fish got battered!

Music Student: "Did you really learn to play the violin in six easy lessons?"
Music Teacher: "Yes, but the 500 that followed were pretty difficult."

What did Noah do for a living?
Preserving pears.

Which animals do you have to beware of
when you take exams?
Cheetahs.

What's a ghost's favorite entertainment?
Going to the phantomime.

"Jimmy, how many more times must I tell you
to come away from that biscuit barrel?"
"No more, mom. It's empty."

1st Witch: "I like your toad. He always has
such a nice expression on his face."
2nd Witch: "It's because he's a hoptimist."

Why did the elephant paint her head yellow?
To see if blondes really do have more fun.

Which vegetable goes best with jacket
potatoes?
Button mushrooms.

What's the difference between a gymnastics teacher and a duck? One goes quick on its legs, the other goes quack on its eggs.

QUACK!

What airline do vampires travel on? British Scareways.

Two fleas were sitting on Robinson Crusoe's back as he lay on the beach in the sun. "Well, so long," said one to the other, "I'll see you on Friday."

Did you hear about the stupid photographer? He saved burned-out light bulbs for use in his darkroom.

Why did the champion monster give up boxing?
He didn't want to spoil his looks.

"Doctor, doctor, I keep seeing double."
"Take a seat, please."
"Which one?"

What's the difference between a nail and a boxer?
One gets knocked in, the other gets knocked out.

What happened when the idiot had a brain transplant?
The brain rejected him.

Two shipwrecked sailors managed to climb onto an iceberg. "Oh, dear," said the first, "do you think we'll survive?"
"Of course we will," said the second. "Look, here comes the *Titanic*."

Two fishermen were out in their boat one day when a hand appeared in the ocean. "What's that?" asked the first fisherman. "It looks as if someone's drowning!"
"Nonsense," said the second. "It was just a little wave."

What did one cannibal say to another?
"Who was that girl I saw you with last night?"
"That was no girl, that was my supper."

What kind of bandage do people wear after heart surgery?
Ticker tape.

What's black and white, black and white, black and white?
A nun rolling down a hill.

What kind of jokes does a chiropodist like?
Corny jokes.

Did you hear about the woman who was so
keen on road safety that she always wore
white at night?
Last winter she was knocked down by a
snow plow.

What did one magician say to another?
"Who was that girl I sawed you with last
night?"

First cannibal woman: "I just don't know
what to make of my husband these days."
Second cannibal woman: "How about a
curry?"

Did you hear about the village idiot buying
bird seed?
He said he wanted to grow some birds.

Did you hear about the boy who got worried
when his nose grew to 11 inches long?
He thought it might turn into a foot.

What was the fly doing in the alphabet soup?
Learning to spell.

"Doctor, doctor, I think I've been bitten by a vampire."
"Drink this glass of water."
"Will it make me better?"
"No, but I'll be able to see if your neck leaks."

How did the Vikings communicate with one another?
By Norse code.

DOT-DOT-DASH

What do you do if you split your sides laughing?
Run until you get a stitch.

How can you tell an old person from a young person?
An old person can sing and brush their teeth at the same time.

What did Enormous Eric win when he lost 50 pounds in weight?
The No-Belly Prize.

Teacher: "Why are you late, Penelope?"
Penelope: "I was obeying the sign that says 'Children – Dead Slow,' Miss."

Whom does a monster ask for a date?
Any old ghoul he can find.

"Mommy, Mommy, I don't like Daddy!"
"Well, just eat the salad then, dear."

How many skunks does it take to make a big stink?
A phew!

What did one skeleton say to the other?
"If we had any guts we'd get out of here."

Why was the man arrested for looking at sets of dentures in a dentist's window?
Because it was against the law to pick your teeth in public.

Where do ghouls go to study?
Ghoullege.

What do you do if your nose goes on strike?
Picket.

Do undertakers enjoy their job?
Of corpse they do.

Teacher: "Didn't you know the bell had gone?"
Silly Sue: "I didn't take it, Miss."

Teacher: "Peter! Why are you scratching yourself?"
Peter: "'Cos no one else knows where I itch."

Teacher: Fred! Wipe that mud off your shoes before you come in the classroom."
Fred: "But, Sir, I'm not wearing any shoes."

Knock, knock.
Who's there?
Sacha.
Sacha who?
Sacha lot of questions in this exam!

There were ten zebras in the zoo. All but nine escaped. How many were left?
Nine!

Teacher: "Who knows what a hippy is?"
Clever Dick: "It's something that holds your leggy on."

Teacher: "Who can tell me what an archaeologist is?"
Tracey: "It's someone whose career is in ruins."

Teacher: "Barbara, name three collective nouns."
Barbara: "The wastepaper bin, the garbage bin and the vacuum cleaner."

Why are pianos so noble?
Because they're either upright or grand.

Hil: "Who was the fastest runner in history?"
Bill: "Adam. He was first in the human race."

What do ghosts do at 11 a.m.?
Take a coffin break.

Why are vampires artistic?
They're good at drawing blood.

Why did Silly Sue throw her guitar away?
Because it had a hole in the middle.

What's the difference between a caretaker
and a bad-tempered teacher?
Is there any difference?

Monica fancied herself as an artist.
But her teacher said she was so bad
it was a wonder she could draw
breath.

Henry: "I'd like to learn to play a drum,
Sir."
Music Teacher: "Beat it!"

Did you hear about Miss Spellbinder's new
twins?
It's difficult to tell witch from witch.

1st Witch: "Every time it's misty, I hear a
strange croaking noise coming from your
house."
2nd Witch: "That would be my frog
horn."

Did you hear about the boy who was told to do 100 lines?
He drew 100 cats on the paper. He thought the teacher had said "lions."

What kind of monster has the best hearing?
The eeriest.

What happened when the Ice Monster ate a curry?
He blew his cool.

What has eight feet and sings?
The school quartet.

"What's your handicrafts teacher like?"
"She's a sew and sew."

Teacher: "What's a robin?"
John: "A bird that steals, Miss."

Which ghost sailed the seven seas looking for rubbish and blubber?
The ghost of BinBag the Whaler.

How can you tell if you've had a elephant in your fridge?
It leaves footprints in the butter.

1st Witch: "My trash can must be full of toadstools."
2nd Witch: "Why's that?"
1st Witch: "There's not mushroom inside."

Witch: "Try some of my sponge cake."
Wizard: "It's a bit tough."
Witch: "That's strange. I only bought the sponge from the drugstore this morning."

Why did the
cyclops apply for
half a television
license?
Because he only
had one eye.

What is black and has eight wheels?
A witch on roller skates.

A man out for a walk came across a little
boy pulling his cat's tail. "Hey, you!" he
called. "Don't pull the cat's tail!"
"I'm not pulling!" replied the little boy. "I'm
only holding on — the cat's doing the pulling!"

How did the invisible boy upset his mother?
He kept appearing.

Did you hear about the stupid monster who hurt himself while he was raking up leaves? He fell out of a tree.

What gets bigger the more you take away? A hole.

Dr Frankenstein decided to build an extension to his laboratory, so he crossed a cement mixer, a ghoul and a chicken. Now he's got a demon bricklayer.

What did the angry monster do when he got his gas bill? He exploded.

Why did the wooden monsters stand in a circle? They were having a board meeting.

What comes out at night and goes "Munch, munch, ouch!" A vampire with a rotten tooth.

Two ghouls were in the middle of an argument. "I didn't come here to be insulted," yelled one.
"Really? Where do you usually go?"

Witch: "I've never been so insulted in my life! I went to a Halloween party, and at midnight they asked me to take my mask off."
Spook: "Why are you so angry?"
Witch: "I wasn't wearing a mask."

What did the shy pebble monster say?
"I wish I was a little boulder."

How do monsters count to 13?
On their fingers.

How do they count to 47?
They take off their socks and count their toes.

Why did the undertaker chop all his corpses into little bits?
Because he liked them to rest in pieces.

1st Monster: "Where do fleas go in winter?"
Werewolf: "Search me!"

Why are most monsters covered in wrinkles?
Have you ever tried to iron a monster?

What is even more invisible than the invisible ghost?
His shadow.

Why do monsters wear glasses?
So that they don't bump into other monsters.

What should you do if a zombie borrows your comic?
Wait for him to give it back.

Why do demons get on so well with ghouls?
Because demons are a ghoul's best friend.

Did you hear the story of the three holes?
Well, well, well.

What is a skeleton?
Someone who went on a diet and forgot to say "when."

The vampire went into the Monster Cafe. "Shark and chips," he ordered. "And make it snappy."

Why was the insect thrown out of the forest?
Because he was a litter bug.

My auntie has a sore throat. What should
she do?
Take auntie-septic.

What did the undertaker say to his
girlfriend?
"Em-balmy about you."

What happened when the pussy swallowed a
dime?
There was money in the kitty.

What does Dracula say to his victims?
"It's been nice gnawing you."

What did the traffic light say to the
motorist?
"Don't look now, I'm changing."

What do ghosts wear if they're short-sighted?
Spooktacles.

"I can't understand why people say my girlfriend's legs look like matchsticks. They do look like sticks – but they certainly don't match."

"What's your dad getting for Christmas?"
"Bald and fat."

Albert Littleun is so small his chin has a rash from his bootlaces.

"Doctor, doctor, I keep thinking I'm a pair of curtains!"
"Pull yourself together, man."

"She's the kind of girl that boys look at twice – they can't believe it the first time."

"Some girls who are the picture of health are just painted that way."

Ghost: "Do you believe in the hereafter?"
Phantom: "Of course I do."
Ghost: "Well, hereafter leave me alone."

Ghost: "I've been invited to an avoidance."
Monster: "An avoidance? What's that?"
Ghost: "It's a dance for people who hate each other."

What did the neurotic pig say to the farmer?
"You take me for grunted."

Waiter: "And how did you find your meat, sir?"
Customer: "Oh, I just lifted a potato and there it was."

Why did Dracula eat strong peppermints?
Because he had bat breath.

How did dinosaurs pass exams?
With extinction.

Why did the lazy idiot apply for a job in a
bakery?
He fancied a long loaf.

"You must think I'm a perfect idiot."
"No, you're not perfect."

Why are Martians green?
Because they forgot to take their travel-
sickness tablets.

"You are so ugly your face would stop a clock."
"And yours would make one run."

Patient: "Tell me honestly, how am I?"
Dentist: "Your teeth are fine, but your gums will have to come out."

"Mom's cooking is improving. The smoke is not as black as it used to be!"

"Yes, I do like your dress – but isn't it a little early for Halloween?"

What did the beaver say to the tree?
It sure is good to gnaw you.

Why was the ghost arrested?
He didn't have a haunting license.

What did the dragon say when he saw St George in his shining armor?
Oh no, not more tinned food.

A catcall is when someone goes out at night saying, "Puss, puss, puss."

How can a teacher double his money?
By folding it in half.

Why did the composer spend all his time in bed?
He wrote sheet music.

Teacher: "Why did the Romans build straight roads?"
Alex: "So the Britons couldn't lie in ambush round the corners."

What is brown, hairy, wears dark glasses and carries a pile of exercise books?
A coconut disguised as a teacher.

What do you call a deaf teacher?
Anything you like, he can't hear you.

How do teachers dress in mid-January?
Quickly.

What's the definition of a good actor?
Somebody who tries hard to be everybody but himself.

Music Teacher: "Do you like opera, Francesca?"
Francesca: "Apart from the singing, yes."

When is the water in the shower room musical?
When it's piping hot.

What takes a lot of licks from a teacher without complaint?
An ice cream.

Did you hear that
Dumb Donald got
splinters in his fingers?
He'd been scratching
his head!

Do men always snore?
No. Only when they're asleep.

School Doctor: "Have you ever had trouble with appendicitis?"
Naomi: "Only when I tried to spell it."

Why did the old lady walk around with her purse open?
She'd read there was going to be some change in the weather.

Did you hear about the spook who went on a high fiber diet?
He had beans on ghost twice a day.

180

Which hand should you use to stir your tea?
Neither – you should use a spoon!

Barbara: "I wish I'd been alive a few hundred years ago."
History Teacher: "Why?"
Barbara: "There'd have been a lot less history to learn."

Teacher: "Write 'I must not forget my gym kit' 100 times."
Nicky: "But, Sir, I only forgot it once."

What kind of musical instrument can you use for fishing?
The cast-a-net.

Science Teacher: "What happened when electricity was first discovered?"
Alex: "Someone got a nasty shock."

Why was Cinderella thrown out of the school's netball team?
Because she kept running away from the ball.

English Teacher: "Now give me a sentence using the word 'fascinate.'"
Clara: "My raincoat has ten buttons but I can only fasten eight."

How can you save school dumplings from drowning?
Put them in gravy boats.

Why did the teacher wear a lifejacket at night?
Because she liked sleeping on a water bed, and couldn't swim!

What's the difference between a crossword expert, a greedy boy and a pot of glue?
A crossword expert is a good puzzler and the greedy boy's a pud guzzler. The pot of glue? Ah, that's where you get stuck.

Countess Dracula: "Say something soft and sweet to me."
Dracula: "Marshmallows, chocolate fudge cake . . ."

Why did the ghost's trousers fall down?
Because he had no visible means of support.

What did the Eskimo schoolboy say to the Eskimo schoolgirl?
"What's an ice girl like you doing in a place like this?"

What can a schoolboy keep and give away at the same time?
A cold.

What's the best way of avoiding infection from biting ghosts?
Don't bite any ghosts.

What's the very lowest game you can play?
Baseball.

"Doctor, doctor, I can't stand being three feet tall any longer."
"Then you'll just have to learn to be a little patient."

Teacher: "Why do birds fly south in winter?"
Jim: "Because it's too far to walk."

Teacher: "Can you say your name backwards, Simon?"
Simon: "No, Mis."

Teacher: "Who can tell me what 'dogma' means?"
Cheeky Charlie: "It's a lady dog that's had puppies, Sir."

What game do little cannibals like to play at parties?
Swallow my leader.

And what game do little ghosts play at parties?
Haunt the thimble.

Knock, knock.
Who's there?
Ida.
Ida who?
Ida nawful time at school today.

What's a cannibal's favorite drink?
Wine with a lot of body.

Knock, knock.
Who's there?
Genoa.
Genoa who?
Genoa good place to eat?

How did the teacher knit a suit of armor?
She used steel wool.

Geography Teacher: "How can you prove that the world is round?"
Ben: "But I never said it was, Sir."

"I'm speechless."
"Good, just stay that way."

"Doctor, doctor, I keep thinking I'm a canary."
"I can't tweet you, go and see a vet."

"My Mom is a beautiful redhead – no hair, just a red head."

"Doctor, doctor, I've only got 50 seconds to live."
"Just sit over there a minute."

Did you hear about the Irish monster who went to night school to learn to read in the dark?

1st Monster: "That orange and red checked coat of yours is a bit loud."
2nd Monster: "It's okay when I put my muffler on."

If you have a referee in football, and an umpire in cricket, what do you have in bowls?
Goldfish.

Father: "Would you like a pocket calculator for Christmas, son?"
Danny: "No thanks, Dad. I know how many pockets I've got."

Why is a complaining brother the easiest to satisfy?
Because nothing satisfies him.

What do you get if you try to take a ghost's photograph?
Transparencies.

Clarrie: "Our math teacher has long black hair all down her back."
Barry: "Yes, it's a pity it doesn't grow on her head."

Who speaks at the ghosts' press conference?
The spooksperson.

What is Count Dracula's favorite snack?
A fangfurter.

Woman: "If you were my husband I'd poison your coffee."
Man: "And if you were my wife, I'd drink it."

What do you get if you cross your least favorite teacher with a telescope?
A horrorscope.

1st Ghost: "I find haunting castles really boring these days."
2nd Ghost: "I know what you mean. I just don't seem to be able to put any life into it."

Why did the monster walk over the hill?
It was too much bother to walk under it.

What's the cannibal's favorite restaurant
called?
Man Alive.

"Joan, pick up your feet when you walk."
"What for, Mom? I've only got to put them
down again."

What do ghosts eat for breakfast?
Dreaded wheat.

What did one ghost say to another?
"I'm sorry, but I just don't believe in
people."

How do ghosts keep their feet dry?
By wearing boo-ts.

Which is the ghost's favorite stretch of
water?
Lake Eerie.

What is a ghost's favorite dessert?
Boo-berry pie with I-scream.

Why are ghosts invisible?
They wear see-through clothes.

What do ghostly soldiers say to strangers?
"Who ghost there?"

Why is the graveyard such a noisy place?
Because of all the coffin!

Waiter on ocean liner: "Would you like the menu, sir?"
Monster: "No thanks, just bring me the passenger list."

What do you do with a green ghost?
Wait until he is ripe.

What do ghosts like about riding horses?
Ghoulloping.

Mrs Monster to Mr Monster: "Try to be nice to my mother when she visits us this weekend, dear. Fall down when she hits you."

What is a ghost's favorite Wild West town?
Tombstone.

Why was Baron Frankenstein never lonely?
Because he was good at making fiends.

What did the ghost real estate agent say to the ghost?
"I'm sorry, sir, we have nothing suitable for you to haunt at the moment."

Why did the ghosts hold a seance?
To try to contact the living.

Which weight do ghosts box at?
Phantom weight.

How does a witch tell the time?
She wears a witch watch.

Mr Monster: "Oi, hurry up with my supper."
Mrs Monster: "Oh, do be quiet – I've only got three pairs of hands."

1st Ghost: "Am I late for dinner?"
2nd Ghoul: "Yes, everyone's been eaten."

Father Monster: "Johnny, don't make faces at that man. I've told you before not to play with your food."

What do you get if you cross a yeti with a kangaroo?
A fur coat with big pockets.

What do you get if you cross an elephant with the abominable snowman?
A jumbo yeti.

What do you call two witches who share a room?
Broom-mates.

Why did the witch put her broom in the washing machine?
She wanted a clean sweep.

What noise does a witch's breakfast cereal make?
Snap, cackle, pop!

"Doctor, doctor, I think I'm a witch!"
"You'd better lie down for a spell."

What do you call a wizard from outer space?
A flying sorcerer.

How can you tell if a vampire has been at your tomato juice?
By the teethmarks on the lid.

Witch in shoe shop: "I'd like a pair of sandals, please."
Shop Assistant: "Certainly, madam, what kind?"
Witch: "Open-toed, of course."

What do you call a motorbike belonging to a witch?
A brrooooom stick.

Why do skeletons drink milk?
Because it's good for the bones.

What do you get if you cross an owl with a
vampire?
A bird that's ugly but doesn't give a hoot.

Why did Mr and Mrs Werewolf call their
son Camera?
Because he was always snapping.

Was Dracula ever married?
No, he was a bat-chelor.

Who has the most dangerous job in
Transylvania?
The dentist.

Why was Dracula so happy at the races?
His horse won by a neck.

What do you get if you cross a vampire with
Al Capone?
A fangster!

How does a vampire enter his house?
Through the bat flap.

Why are skeletons usually so calm?
Nothing gets under their skin.

What do you call a skeleton who's always
telling lies?
A bony phoney.

What do vampires gamble with?
Stake money.

How did skeletons send each other letters in
the days of the Wild West?
By Bony Express.

What do you get if you cross a vampire with a mummy?
A flying bandage.

Why was Dracula always willing to help young vampires?
Because he liked to see new blood in the business.

What happens to a witch when she loses her temper?
She flies off the handle.

Why do skeletons hate winter?
Because the cold goes right through them.

What do you get if you cross a vampire with a car?
A monster that attacks vehicles and sucks out all their gas.

What do you call an old and foolish vampire?
A silly old sucker.

How does a vampire get through life with only one fang?
He has to grin and bare it.

What is Count Dracula's favorite pudding?
Leeches and scream.

If a boxer was knocked out by Dracula, what would he be?
Out for the Count.

Who is a vampire likely to fall in love with?
The girl necks door.

What do you call a boy with a car on his head?
Jack.

What is red, sweet and bites people in the neck?
A jampire.

Mrs Vampire: "Will you still love me when I'm old and ugly?"
Mr Vampire: "Darling, of course I do."

What's the difference between a vampire with toothache and a rainstorm?
One roars with pain and the other pours with rain.

How do you survive
the electric chair?
Insulate you
underpants.

How do you make a vampire float?
Take two scoops of ice cream, a glass of Coke and add one vampire.

Why did the vampire actress turn down so many film offers?
She was waiting for a part she could get her teeth into.

What do you get if you cross a midget with Dracula?
A vampire that sucks blood from your kneecaps.

Did you hear about the doctor who crossed a parrot with a vampire?
It bit his neck, sucked his blood and said, "Who's a pretty boy then?"

Father: "I want to take my girl out of this terrible math class."
Teacher: "But she's top of the class."
Father: "That's why I think it must be a terrible class."

What is Dracula's favorite breed of dog?
The bloodhound.

What's a vampire's worst enemy?
Fang decay.

What is bright red and dumb?
A blood clot.

1st Vampire: "I don't think much of your sister's neck."
2nd Vampire: "Never mind – eat the vegetables instead."

What is ugly, scary and very blue?
A vampire holding his breath.

What do you get if you cross a vampire with a flea?
Lots of very worried dogs.

Girl: "Mom, you know you're always worried about me failing math?"
Mother: "Yes."
Girl: "Well, your worries are over."

Did you hear about the stupid water-polo player?
His horse drowned . . .

Mother: "Did you get a good place in the geography test?"
Daughter: "Yes, Mom, I sat next to the cleverest kid in the class."

Teacher: "Colin, one of your essays is very good but the other one I can't read."
Colin: "Yes, sir. My mother is a much better writer than my father."

What kind of snake is useful on your window?
A viper.

"It's a note from the teacher about me telling lies – but it's not true."

Girl: "My teacher's a peach."
Mother: "You mean she's sweet."
Girl: "No, she has a heart of stone."

Teacher to pupil: "How many thousand times have I told you not to exaggerate?"

Why don't astronauts get hungry after being blasted into space?
Because they've just had a big launch.

Jennifer: "How come you did so badly in history? I thought you had all the dates written on your sleeve."

Miriam: "That's the trouble, I put on my geography blouse by mistake."

Teacher: "How many make a dozen?"
Boy: "Twelve."
Teacher: "Correct. And how many make a million?"
Boy: "Dad says very few."

Mother: "How was your first day at school?"
Little Boy: "Okay, but I haven't got my present yet."
Mother: "What do you mean?"
Little Boy: "Well the teacher gave me a chair, and said, 'Sit there for the present.'"

How do pixies eat?
By gobblin.

What did the little eye say to the big eye?
"Aye, aye, Captain!"

What do you get if you cross a cow and a camel?
Lumpy milkshakes!

What do you get if you cross a sheep dog and a bunch of daisies?
Collie-flowers!

What do you get if you cross an elephant and peanut butter?
Either peanut butter that never forgets, or an elephant that sticks to the roof of your mouth.

What do you get if you cross a zebra and a donkey?
A zeedonk.

What do you get if you cross a kangaroo and a mink?
A fur jumper with pockets.

Who makes suits and eats spinach?
Popeye the Tailorman.

What do you get if you cross a sheep and a rainstorm?
A wet blanket.

What do you get if you cross a centipede and a parrot?
A walkie-talkie.

How do you make gold soup?
Use fourteen carats.

Why did the orange stop rolling down the hill?
It ran out of juice.

What goes ninety-nine donk, ninety-nine donk?
A centipede with a wooden leg.

If King Kong went to Hong Kong to play ping-pong and died, what would they put on his coffin?
A lid.

"Why are you taking that steel wool home?"
"I'm going to knit myself a car."

Did you hear about the stupid tap dancer?
He fell in the sink.

What do you get if you cross a cat with a canary?
A cat with a full tummy.

Where does Tarzan buy his clothes?
At a Jungle Sale.

What lives in a pod and is a Kung Fu
expert?
Bruce Pea.

What's big, hairy and can fly?
King Koncorde.

What kind of cans are there in Mexico?
Mexicans.

What is yellow and goes click-click?
A ballpoint banana.

Have you heard the joke about the wall?
You'd never get over it.

What can you make that can't be seen?
A noise.

What has four eyes and a mouth?
The Mississippi.

How do you get rid of varnish?
Take away the R.

What fish do dogs chase?
Catfish.

If a crocodile makes shoes, what does a
banana make?
Slippers.

What is it that even the most careful person
overlooks?
His nose.

What is a tornado?
Mother Nature doing the twist.

What pet makes the loudest noise?
A trum-pet.

What is full of holes but can hold water?
A sponge.

What makes the Tower of Pisa lean?
It doesn't eat much.

What do you get if you cross a worm with a young goat?
A dirty kid.

Will you remember me in one day's time?
Of course I will.
Will you remember me in a week's time?
Of course I will.
Will you remember me in a year's time?
Of course I will.
Will you remember me in ten years' time?
Of course I will.
Knock, knock.
Who's there?
See — you've forgotten already!

"I bet I can make you speak like a Red Indian."
"How?"
"That's right!"

Knock, knock.
Who's there?
Howard.
Howard who?
Howard you like to stand out here in the cold while some idiot keeps saying "Who's there . . .?"

"Why are you laughing?"
"My silly dentist just pulled one of my teeth out."
"I don't see much to laugh about in that."
"Ah, but it was the wrong one!"

Knock, knock.
Who's there?
Olive.
Olive who?
Olive across the road.

Knock, knock.
Who's there?
Fanny.
Fanny who?
Fanny the way you keep saying "Who's there?"

Knock, knock.
Who's there?
Little old lady.
Little old lady who?
I didn't know you could yodel.

How many days of the week start with the letter T?
Four: Tuesday, Thursday, today and tomorrow.

"My brother's been practising the violin for ten years."
"Is he any good?"
"No. It was nine years before he found out he wasn't supposed to blow it."

"Is this a second-hand shop?"
"Yes, sir."
"Good. Can you fit one on my watch, please?"

"In the park this morning I was surrounded by lions."
"Lions! In the park?"
"Yes – dandelions!"

"How's your business coming along?"
"I'm looking for a new cashier."
"But you only had a new one last week."
"That's the one I'm looking for."

"I'll lend you a dollar if you promise not to keep it too long."
"Oh, I won't. I'll spend it right away."

"Are you superstitious?"
"No."
"Then lend me $13".

"A pound of kiddies, please, butcher."
"You mean a pound of kidneys."
"That's what I said, diddie I?"

What do zombies play?
Corpses and robbers.

"Have you any invisible ink?"

"Certainly, sir. What color?"

An extremely tall man with round shoulders, very long arms and one leg six inches shorter than the other went into a tailor's shop.

"I'd like to see a suit that will fit me," he told the tailor.

"So would I, sir," the tailor sympathized. "So would I."

At the seaside, Mom waxed all lyrical at the beauty of the sunset over the sea.

"Doesn't the sun look wonderful setting on to the horizon?" she breathed.

"Yes," said young Sammy, "and there won't half be a fizz when it touches the water!"

"What did you get for Christmas?"
"A mouth-organ. It's the best present I ever got."
"Why?"
"My mom gives me 50 cents a week not to blow it."

"What do you mean by telling everyone I'm an idiot?"
"I'm sorry. I didn't know it was supposed to be a secret."

At the scene of a bank raid the policeman came running up to the officer and said, "He got away, sir!"
The officer was furious. "But I told you to put a man on all the exits!" he roared. "How could he have got away?"
"He left by one of the entrances, sir!"

As two boys were passing the vicarage, the vicar leaned over the wall and showed them a ball. "Is this yours?" he asked.
"Did it do any damage, vicar?" said one of the boys.
"No," replied the vicar.
"Then it's mine."

"Good morning, sir. I'm applying for the job as handyman."

"I see. Well, are you handy?"

"Couldn't be more so. I only live next door."

"What do you think of this photograph of me?"

"It makes you look older, frankly."

"Oh well, it'll save the cost of having another one taken later on."

"My brother's just opened a shop."

"Really? How's he doing?"

"Six months. He opened it with a crowbar."

At a party, a magician was producing egg after egg from a little boy's ear.

"There!" he said proudly. "I bet your Mom can't produce eggs without hens, can she?"

"Oh yes, she can," said the boy, "she keeps ducks."

A noise woke me up this morning.

What was that?

The crack of dawn.

What kind of ant is good at adding up?
An accountant.

This match won't light.
That's funny — it did this morning.

"It can't go on! It can't go on!"
"What can't go on?"
"This baby's vest — it's too small for me."

"It's gone forever — gone forever I tell you."
"What has?"
"Yesterday."

"Mom, you know that vase that's been handed down from generation to generation?"
"Yes."
"Well, this generation's dropped it."

As the judge said to the dentist: "Do you swear to pull the tooth, the whole tooth, and nothing but the tooth?"

A man in a swimming pool was on the very top diving board. He poised, lifted his arms, and was about to dive when the attendant came running up, shouting,
"Don't dive — there's no water in that pool!"
"That's all right," said the man. "I can't swim!"

"Just think — a big chocolate ice-cream, a bag of scrumptious toffees, and a seat at the cinema for 50 cents."
"Did you get all that for 50 cents?"
"No — but just think . . . !"

"I wonder where I got that puncture."
"Maybe it was at that last fork in the road . . ."

"My uncle's got a wooden leg."
"That's nothing. My auntie has a wooden chest."

Did you hear about the girl who got engaged to a chap and then found out he had a wooden leg?
She broke it off, of course . . .

"Waiter, waiter, there's a bird in my soup."
"That's all right, sir. It's bird-nest soup."

Passer-by (to fisherman): "Is this river any good for fish?"
Fisherman: "It must be. I can't get any of them to leave it."

Vegetarian: "I've lived on nothing but vegetables for years."
Bored listener: "That's nothing. I've lived on Earth all my life."

"Waiter, waiter, this coffee tastes like mud."
"I'm not surprised, sir, it was ground only a few minutes ago."

"Waiter, waiter, does the pianist play requests?"
"Yes, sir"
"Then ask him to play tiddledywinks until I've finished my meal."

There once was a writer named Wright,
Who instructed his son to write right;
He said, "Son, write Wright right.
It's not right to write
Wright as 'rite' – try to write Wright all right!"

"Waiter, waiter, your tie is in my soup!"
"That's all right, sir. It's not shrinkable."

A charming young singer named Hannah,
Got caught in a flood in Savannah;
As she floated away,
Her sister, they say,
Accompanied her on the piannah!

"You've got your socks on inside out."
"I know, Mom, but there are holes on the
other side."

"How did your mom know you hadn't
washed your face?"
"I forgot to wet the soap."

What dog smells of onions?
A hot dog.

"Dad, is an ox a sort of male cow?"
"Sort of, yes."
"And equine means something to do with horses, doesn't it?"
"That's right."
"So what's an equinox?"

"What's the matter?" one man asked another.
"My wife left me when I was in the bath last night," sobbed the second man.
"She must have been waiting for years for the chance," replied the first.

What lies on the ground 100 feet up in the air and smells?
A dead centipede.

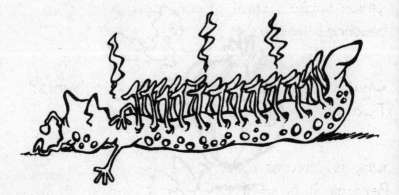

"Five dollars for one question!" said the woman to the fortune teller.
"That's very expensive, isn't it?"
"Next!"

Who is the biggest gangster in the sea?
Al Caprawn.

"Mom, can I have two pieces of cake, please?"
"Certainly – take this piece and cut it in two!"

"Don't eat the biscuits so fast – they'll keep."
"I know, but I want to eat as many as I can before I lose my appetite."

Which soldiers smell of salt and pepper?
Seasoned troopers.

What's green, has four legs and two trunks?
Two seasick tourists.

Why is perfume obedient?
Because it is scent wherever it goes.

Visitor: "You're very quiet, Jennifer."
Jennifer: "Well, my mom gave me 50 cents not to say anything about your red nose."

What illness did everyone on the Enterprise catch?
Chicken Spocks.

What's black and white, pongs and hangs from a line?
A drip-dry skunk.

An irate customer in a restaurant complained that his fish was bad, so the waiter picked it up, smacked it and said, "Naughty, naughty, naughty!"

What do you call a man with cow droppings all over his shoes?
An incowpoop.

What did the grape do when the elephant sat on it?
It let out a little wine.

He's so stupid he thinks Camelot is where Arabs park their camels.

What do you get if you cross a nun and a chicken?
A pecking order.

Where do snowmen go to dance?
A snowball.

What does Luke Skywalker shave with?
A laser blade.

What do frogs drink?
Croaka-Cola.

What happens when a frog's car breaks down?
It gets toad away.

Who is in cowboy films and is always broke?
Skint Eastwood.

What's the fastest thing in water?
A motor-pike.

Why did the idiot have his sundial floodlit?
So he could tell the time at night.

Which capital city cheats at exams?
Peking.

Why did the skeleton run up a tree?
Because a dog was after its bones.

What do you call a flea that lives in an idiot's ear?
A space invader.

What do ants take when they are ill?
Antibiotics.

Why was the Egyptian girl worried?
'Cos her Daddy was a mummy.

What did the spider say
to the beetle?
"Stop bugging me."

Why did the woman take a load of hay to
bed?
To feed her nightmare.

Who said "Shiver me timbers!" on the ghost
ship?
The skeleton crew.

What do cats prefer for breakfast?
Mice Crispies.

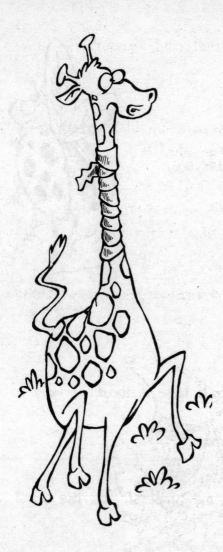

What's worse
than a giraffe
with a sore
throat?
A centipede
with athlete's
foot.

What is the best thing to take into the desert?
A thirst-aid kit.

What has webbed feet and fangs?
Count Quackula.

Why is a turkey like an evil little creature?
'Cos it's always a-gobblin' . . .

Why did the skeleton go the party?
For a rattling good time!

What do you call a highwayman who is ill?
Sick Turpin.

"Bring me a crocodile sandwich immediately."
"I'll make it snappy, sir."

What did the tie say to the hat?
"You go on ahead and I'll hang around."

What did the picture say to the wall?
"I've got you covered."

Where does a general keep his armies?
Up his sleevies.

What swings through trees and is very dangerous?
A chimpanzee with a machine gun.

Who was the first underwater spy?
James Pond.

How do you milk a mouse?
You can't – the bucket won't fit under it.

What is hairy and coughs?
A coconut with a cold.

What's the fastest cake in the world?
Meriiiiiiiiiiiiiingue.

What do you call a foreign body in a chip pan?
An Unidentified Frying Object.

When is it bad luck to be followed by a black cat?
When you're a mouse.

What cake wanted to rule the world?
Attila the Bun.

How did Noah see the animals in the Ark?
By floodlighting.

What do cannibals eat for breakfast?
Buttered host.

What has four legs, whiskers, a tail, and flies?
A dead cat.

How does an elephant go up a tree?
It stands on an acorn and waits for it to grow.

"Have you ever seen a man-eating tiger?"
"No, but in the café next door I once saw a man eating chicken!"

"I'll have to report you, sir," said the traffic cop to the speeding driver. "You were doing 85 miles an hour."
"Nonsense, officer," declared the driver. "I've only been in the car for ten minutes!"

What lies at the bottom of the sea and
shivers?
A nervous wreck.

Why did the man take a pencil to bed?
To draw the curtains . . .
I'd tell you another joke about a pencil, but
it hasn't any point.

Why does an
ostrich have such
a long neck?
Because its head
is so far from its
body.

Why did the burglar take a shower?
He wanted to make a clean getaway.

Why do idiots eat biscuits?
Because they're crackers.

What do you call an American drawing?
Yankee Doodle.

Why do bears wear fur coats?
They'd look silly in plastic macs.

What do you call a mayfly with a machine gun?
A baddy-long-legs.

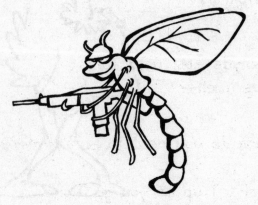

What's a mermaid?
A deep-she fish.

What is cowhide most used for?
Holding cows together.

What training do you need to be a garbage collector?
None, you pick it up as you go along.

Did you hear about the sword swallower
who swallowed an umbrella?
He wanted to put something away for a
rainy day.

"Would you like to play with our new dog?"
"He looks very fierce. Does he bite?"
"That's what I want to find out."

Did you hear about the granny who plugged
her electric blanket into the toaster by
mistake?
She spent the night popping out of bed.

"What's your new dog's name?"
"Dunno — he won't tell me."

First cat: "How did you get on in the milk-drinking contest?"
Second cat: "Oh, I won by six laps!"

Andy was late for school. "Andy!" roared his mother. "Have you got your socks on yet?"
"Yes, Mom," replied Andy. "All except one."

Why did the lizard go on a diet?
It weighed too much for its scales.

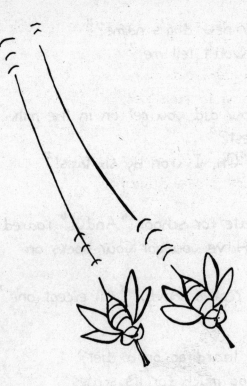

"Doctor, doctor, I don't like all these flies buzzing around my head."
"Pick out the ones you like and I'll swat the rest."

"Millicent! What did I say I'd do if I found you with your fingers in the butter again?"
"That's funny, Mom. I can't remember either."

"My wife says that if I don't give up golf
she'll leave me."
"Say, that's tough, old man."
"Yeah, I'm going to miss her."

Where is Dracula's office in America?
In the Vampire State Building.

Who carries a sack and bites people?
Santa Jaws.

Doctor: "You seem to be in excellent health, Mrs Brown. Your pulse is as steady and regular as clockwork."
Mrs Brown: "That's because you've got your hand on my watch."

Knock, knock.
Who's there?
Sonia.
Sonia who?
Sonia shoe. I can smell it from here.

Mandy had a puppy on a lead. She met Sandy and said, "I just got this puppy for my little brother."
"Really?" said Sandy. "Whoever did you find to make a swap like that?"

What were the Chicago gangster's last words?
"Who put that violin in my violin case?"

Why are fried onions like a photocopying machine?
They keep repeating themselves.

What do you call an American with a lavatory on his head?
John.

"What's the difference between a Peeping Tom and someone who's just got out of the bath?"
"One is rude and nosy. The other is nude and rosy."

Cannibal in restaurant: "I don't think much of your chef."

Waiter: "In that case, just eat the pudding."

Darren came home with two black eyes and a face covered in blood. His mother was horrified. "You've been fighting," she said. "Who did this to you?"

"I don't know his name," replied Darren. "But I'd know him if I met him again. I've got half his left ear in my pocket."

Cannibal to his daughter: "Now you are nearly old enough to be married, we must start looking around for an edible bachelor."

Why did the teacher put corn in his shoes? Because he had pigeon toes.

"Waiter, waiter, there's a fly in my soup!"
"Don't worry, sir, the spider in the butter will catch it."

What did one virus say to another?
Stay away, I think I've got penicillin.

Why did the child take a sledgehammer to school?
It was the day they broke up.

What makes an ideal present for a monster?
Five pairs of gloves – one for each hand.

What's the name for a short-legged tramp?
A low-down bum.

A naughty child was irritating all the
passengers on the flight from London to New
York. At last one man could stand it no
longer. "Hey kid," he shouted, "why don't you
go outside and play?"

How do you cure a headache?
Put your head through a window, and the
pane will disappear.

When the cow fell over the cliff, little Sarah
couldn't stop laughing. After all, there was
no point in crying over spilled milk.